On the Subject of Kittens and Mittens

★ **A Strange Space™ Novella** ★

KATIE SILVERWINGS

Memphis, TN

PEPTALK PRODUCTIONS, LLC

Publisher's Cataloging-in-Publication Data
provided by Five Rainbows Cataloging Services

Names: Silverwings, Katie, 1991- author.
Title: On the subject of kittens and mittens : a strange space novella / Katie Silverwings.
Description: Memphis, TN : PepTalk Productions, 2024. | Series: Strange space adventures, bk. 6.
Identifiers: LCCN 2024923645 (print) | ISBN 978-1-959922-30-8 (paperback) | ISBN 978-1-959922-31-5 (hardcover) | ISBN 978-1-959922-33-9 (ebook) | ISBN 978-1-959922-32-2 (audiobook)
Subjects: LCSH: Outer space--Fiction. | Family--Fiction. | Extraterrestrial beings--Fiction. | Novellas. | Science fiction. | Snow--Fiction. | BISAC: FICTION / Science Fiction / Action & Adventure. | FICTION / Science Fiction / Alien Contact. | FICTION / Family Life / General. | GSAFD: Science fiction.
Classification: LCC PS3619.I58 O58 2024 (print) | LCC PS3619.I58 (ebook) | DDC 813/.6--dc23.

Published by PepTalk Productions, LLC 2024
Memphis, Tennessee, USA
www.PepTalkProductionsLLC.com

To my own wonderfully warm family, snowballs and all.

Books by Katie Silverwings

FEATHERED FRIENDSHIP
✶ A Strange Space™ Novella ✶

CELADON
✶ A Strange Space™ Novel ✶

HOW OCEAN MERLANI STOLE THEIR NAVIGATOR
✶ A Strange Space™ Novel ✶

WARMTH AND DARKNESS
✶ A Strange Space™ Novella ✶

THE GARDEN IN THE DARKNESS
✶ A Strange Space™ Novel ✶

TALES OF THE NAVIGATORS: VOLUME 1
✶ Strange Space™ Short Stories ✶

ON THE SUBJECT OF KITTENS AND MITTENS
✶ A Strange Space™ Novella ✶

The printing of this edition of *On the Subject of Kittens and Mittens* was made possible through the generous support of the members of the Strange Space™ Fan Club, including:

Astral Navigator

Sharon T. Hinton

Space Adventurer (1 Year)

Tabitha

Thank you so much to all of my Fan Club members and supporters! I couldn't do this without you.

To find out more about the Strange Space™ Fan Club and join for free, visit:

www.KatieSilverwings.com/Fan-Club

Characters Appearing in this Story

The following list of characters is divided by species and arranged in order of their appearance in the narrative. Only characters with significant "speaking roles" have been detailed here. All others present are listed as a group for the reader's reference; characters who are mentioned but do not appear are not included.

Humans

Taimri Hämäläinen
She/her. Also known as "Tam." Ranger co-captain of LSRV *Atascosa*. Counterpart of **River Myrval.** Wife of **George Barker** and adoptive mother of **Sky Miradyn, Ocean Merlani,** and **Storm Melbryl.**

George Barker
He/Him. Lead Tactical Piloting Instructor, Alpha Centauri-New West Space Service Academy. Husband of **Taimri Hämäläinen** and adoptive father of **Ocean Merlani, Sky Miradyn,** and **Storm Melbryl.**

Thomas E. Milland
He/Him. A graduate student in Exoplanetary Geology at the Proxima-West Institute for Science and Technology.

Other Humans Appearing
Pilot-Cadets Noble, Ionescu, Gravener, Kirsch, and Halpern. Field Medicine Cadet Kells.

Florivans

RIVER MYRVAL

They/them. Also called "Jokeni" by their counterpart. Ranger co-captain of LSRV *Atascosa*. Counterpart of **Taimri Hämäläinen.** Entile of **Sky Miradyn, Ocean Merlani,** and **Storm Melbryl.**

SKY MIRADYN BARKER-HÄMÄLÄINEN

They/them. Also known as "Mir." Adopted kitten of **George Barker** and **Taimri Hämäläinen.** Nibling of **River Myrval** and littermate of **Ocean Merlani** and **Storm Melbryl.**

STORM MELBRYL BARKER-HÄMÄLÄINEN

They/them. Also known as "Mel" or "Melppu." Adopted kitten of **George Barker** and **Taimri Hämäläinen.** Nibling of **River Myrval** and littermate of **Sky Miradyn** and **Ocean Merlani.**

OCEAN MERLANI BARKER-HÄMÄLÄINEN

They/them. Also known as "Mer" or "Merlakka." Adopted kitten of **George Barker** and **Taimri Hämäläinen.** Nibling of **River Myrval** and littermate of **Sky Miradyn** and **Storm Melbryl.**

CONTENTS

On the Subject of Kittens and Mittens

✦ A Strange Space™ Novella ✦

KATIE SILVERWINGS

T HERE ARE FAR MORE STARS IN THE GALAXY THAN any sapient creature could reasonably be expected to fathom outside the realm of complex mathematics.

Among these near-uncountable stars, the vast majority are accompanied on their ages-long gravitational dances by entire companies of planets and their satellites. On some of these celestial bodies, be they planets themselves or the moons which encircle them, the conditions sooner or later become right for complex life of infinite variety and character to form.

A few particularly fascinating varieties of this life hail from the system whose star the local sapients have settled on calling *Sol*. These include not only the spacefaring humans and the ice-swimming Europans, but a multitude of other wonderful and curious creatures which evolved alongside them.

Another notable example of sapient life has, within living memory, integrated their society into that of these first two. These are the Florivans: a genderless, vaguely humanoid species whose true origin remains obscure by their own choice, but whose last settled planet had been a remarkably Earth-like one in the Procyon system, roughly 11.4 light-years away from Sol. Humanity's nearest interstellar neighbors became its dearest friends from the day the two species made contact.

The same could not be said of the Novan Imperium, who had introduced themselves as would-be conquerors and drawn humanity into an interstellar war. The War ended with the Novans retreating in the face of an even more powerful alliance of other Galactic Powers and the entire uninhabited fifty-light-year-wide swath of the galaxy surrounding Sol and Procyon ceded to the combined society of the sapients living there. Ending it, though, had cost the Florivans dearly: the Novans had destroyed their Sanctuary planet, and with it all but a fraction of their already-small population.

Some decades after the War, though, all is once again peaceful in the seven star systems that make up the inhabited territory of the Sol Coalition.

It is equally peaceful on a particular moon in orbit of the largest planet in the Alpha Centauri triad. The planet is known as Toliman's Jewel, a grand super gas giant with distinctive green and orange bands of clouds named after the proper name for Alpha Centauri B, the star of the system's three which it circles. The moon in question is

Jewel's largest, and called in turn Toliman's Hideaway. This more Earth-like of the two largest moons among the dozens of satellites hosted by the gas giant is well known for its pleasant range of cool climates and primordial biosphere. Outside of two small cities near the moon's equator, one on either side of the ocean which separates its two largest landmasses, and a few dozen scattered research complexes, Hideaway is by a great majority a nature preserve. Hideaway's sibling moon, Toliman's Workshop, is a slightly smaller analogue to Mars, and host to a single domed metropolis and one of the system's major shipyards.

The region of snow-covered upper foothills of a slowly growing mountain range on the eastern side of Hideaway's smallest land mass is famous for its geothermal activity. Outside of Earth, there are very few places in the Coalition's inhabited worlds with such a high concentration of active geothermal features which are also relatively pleasant and safe. Hideaway's proximity to Jewel's gravitational pull encourages the whole of the moon to be highly geologically active, but most of its other geothermal sites are quite dangerous to human visitors. Generations of exoplanetary geologists have spent countless hours mapping and cataloging the unique mineral formations of these mountains, naturally, as have xenobiologists the collection of native life forms which call them home.

Somewhere in these mountains, cheerful plumes of steam rise from the various small hot springs which bubble up from deep below the snow-covered alien forest and the streams leading down towards the grand river which separates the mountain range from the continent's interior desert. Long before the Novan War, a traveler's lodge and research complex was built halfway into the hillside above one of the cooler and most stable of these springs of mineral-rich water. The various buildings are all in the Neo-Bavarian style preferred by the local architects of the time. The stone components of the half-timbered facades were hewn from the mountains themselves, although these are now neatly concealed by a smooth coating of dura-plaster and paint. The timbers were cut from the quick-growing variety of the tall, pink-barked native trees which make up the majority of the surrounding forest. These beams now stand out from the plastered stone as shimmering lines of black in the daylight and reflect the light of the gas giant which fills the greater portion of the sky at night, seeming almost to glow from within.

On this particular crisp morning, in one of the communal spring-water-bathing areas set up in a private courtyard of the lodge, a pair of Rangers are enjoying a well-deserved vacation from their duties as peacekeepers and emergency service responders.

These are the co-Captains of LSRV *Atascosa*, one of the dozens of tiny, swift-flying starships the Lone Star Ranger Corps uses to get the rest of its personnel where they need to be almost as soon as they're called upon. Unlike the bigger non-Ranger starships, *Atascosa*'s true crew is only made up of her two Rangers. Anyone else who flies with her comes aboard temporarily for the sake of one mission or another. Although the ship is designed to be able to land easily as needed, in this case she's docked at the nearby Alpha Centauri-New West Space Station. While technicians from Workshop's shipyard and the ACNW Space Service Academy make updates and repairs to her systems, *Atascosa*'s Rangers are taking full advantage of their downtime.

One of *Atascosa*'s Rangers currently soaking in the spring pool is the human Taimri Hämäläinen, a tall, deceptively slender woman whose ash-blonde hair is neatly wrapped up in the towel on top of her head to keep it out of the water. The other is the Florivan River Myrval, a shorter-than-average and light grayish-blue example of their silver-striped species. In form, Florivans are not entirely dissimilar to humans, although they feature a second pair of arms below the first, a third eye in the center of their foreheads, long tufted prehensile tails, and large catlike ears atop their heads. Myrval has their long silver hair arranged in a towel just as their counterpart has hers, although in such a way as to leave their ears exposed. Also like Taimri, everything below their upper pair of shoulders is submerged in the warm, soothing water of the hot spring.

It's been a long time indeed since the two of them had an extended break from their work like this. As *Atascosa*'s Captains, they carry the responsibilities of Rangers and those of a starship's all-important Nav/Quan pair at the same time. To that end, Myrval is making a point of *savoring* the downtime, even if they would have chosen a far different place to take their vacation if it had been entirely up to them.

Soaking in the warmth of the lodge's hot springs is a nice way to clear away all of the lingering stress from the past year's worth of Ranger business, for sure. The soothing mineral-rich waters even seem to be helping ease out the lingering stiffness and nerve twinges from Myrval's right leg—the last vestiges of an injury they'd suffered the year before during one of the more intense cases they and their counterpart had become involved in closing.

Yes, Myrval muses to themself, *this is far better than any heat pack.* Under the water, their lower-right hand absently rubs over the long scar on the outside of their affected knee. It's pleasing not to feel a twinge all the way along the mostly-healed nerve in response, for a change. They can't help hoping that the therapeutic effect of the hot springs will be a lasting one.

"So," Taimri asks, breaking the bubbling stillness of the otherwise empty courtyard, "how long do you think it'll *really* take the cadets to make this hike George has them on?"

"Oh..." The wind-chime after-tones of Myrval's voice drift over the water as they wave their long prehensile tail's soggy silver tuft back and forth in the air above the water while they think it over. A few droplets of water splash back into the spring pool. "From what I remember of the route they're supposed to be taking... Four more days, I'd wager? Assuming George doesn't let them get lost and need us to come in for a rescue first, that is. Why?"

"Oh, just thinking." Taimri chuckles and stretches out her arms before placing both of her hands behind her head. She leans back contentedly once more against one of the large stones forming the border of the spring pool. "That gives *us* a few more days to relax with the kittens before this place is full of excitable young pilots."

"I'm just glad that we're staying somewhere *warm.*" Myrval shakes their head, rolling all three of their large golden eyes for punctuation. "If spending two weeks out in a tent in the *snow* with that husband of yours had been part of the deal, I'd have stayed up at the spacedock with *Atascosa* and left this little 'vacation mission' to you."

The absent husband in question, one George Barker, had been a darter pilot in the Sol Coalition Defense Fleet during the War. He likely would have spent the rest of his life as a pilot, too, if not for Myrval's littermate, Ocean Marbree. For reasons Myrval never quite understood, Marbree had *insisted* that George become their counterpart from the first moment they encountered him. Somehow, even though Marbree was barely old enough to be out of their apprenticeship and George was hardly fully grown himself, their parent had allowed it. More than that, their parent had gone so far as to *adopt* him. Never being one to do anything by halves, their parent had made a point of adopting the entirety of the notoriously troublesome squadron he'd belonged to along with him. Myrval had no choice but to accept their littermate's choice of humans and career paths after that.

Myrval had eventually forgiven the man for existing and therefore luring Marbree away from their side, of course; they'd never have met Taimri otherwise. Their acceptance of George as a part of their family has never stopped them from snarking at him whenever they get the chance, although over the years their teasing has grown far more affectionate than it used to be.

Marbree had been one of the few Florivans who stayed with the Fleet after the War, too, and kept George for their Navigator—although *why* they put up with him at all when he was still young and chaotic and prone to getting himself into trouble always baffled Myrval. Still, their beloved littermate was happy with George, and in the end, *that* was the thing that mattered.

Since Marbree's unfortunate death, though, George is neither Pilot nor Astral Navigator, but an instructor in both subjects at the ACNW Space Service Academy. His duties, for reasons Myrval doesn't quite understand, extend to leading his students on survival training excursions at least twice a year. The fact, therefore, remains that it's *George's* fault that they've found themself taking their vacation on this particular moon and staying in a lodge on a frozen mountain. Nice, soothing hot springs or no, they still know who to blame for how cold the rest of the place is.

"You'd have been lonely and bored silly, Jokeni, and you know it." Taimri nudges them knowingly.

"I... *might* have." Myrval shakes a little more of the water off of the tuft of their tail in her direction. Their counterpart's affectionate use of the nickname she gave them not long after they first asked her to take their compact makes them smile: in her native language, it means 'my river', a delightful pun on Myrval's public name if there ever was one.

"Besides! It's not that cold here, comparatively, yes?"

"Not to *you*, Tam, considering how much like your homeland this is—but need I remind you that *your* species is the fully warm-blooded one?" Myrval lifts one of their four arms out of the warmth of the water just long enough to nudge her back.

"I remember." Taimri lets out another chuckle. "At least I've brought you somewhere with warm water to soak in this time?"

Myrval is about to say something dreadfully witty in response, but they're interrupted by a trio of cheerful voices from the other side of the courtyard.

"Entile River! Äiti!" Three young, excited Florivans scamper over to the side of the spring pool. The taller kittens lead the third, smaller one by their upper pair of hands. These are Myrval's beloved niblings: Sky Miradyn, Storm Melbryl, and little Ocean Merlani.

Each of the kittens is a unique shade of silver-striped blue and dressed in a different color of thick four-armed cable-knit sweater to go with their cozy black trousers and house-slippers. Miradyn is the lightest and bluest, with a bright pink sweater and a large matching bow tied in their hair behind their ears. Melbryl, dressed in purple, shares Myrval's own grey-toned blue, albeit a bit darker. Little Merlani, deep blue-green and a full head shorter than their siblings, is sporting an oversized white sweater layered over the top of their better-fitting yellow one; the too-long sleeves of the white sweater are scrunched up so their small four-fingered hands can peek out, while its hem hangs down past their knees.

As is common among their people, the kitten's public names are each in honor of the long-departed members of the family their coloring most resembles. As soon as they were big enough to show patches of skin through their fur, Marbree had named Miradyn's for their older sibling, Sky Laryven, who'd fallen with the rest of SCV *Athene's* crew at the first Battle of the Teegarden Expanse and Melbryl for their parent, who'd been the last Eldest of their people at Procyon's Sanctuary.

Merlani hadn't even opened their eyes yet when the accident happened. When they were finally ready to receive their public name, there was no question of what it would be. In Myrval's opinion, the youngest generation of their family are perfect miniatures of their lost loved ones. It's bittersweet, sometimes, to know the kittens will never meet their namesakes, but the flashes of similar traits they show now and again bring Myrval no end of joy. The memories are worth the pain to keep.

These kittens are Myrval and Taimri's responsibility for the moment, although usually George is the one in charge of them. His life at AC-NW is far more stable and safe for growing kittens, after all. A two-week-long survival training hike through snowy mountain forests, however, is *hardly* a place for a trio of enthusiastically curious Florivan kittens—even if their adoptive father is the one leading the hike.

"Hello, kittens!" calls Taimri, waving fondly to her adopted children. "Did you need some help with your lesson packs after all?"

"We finished our lesson packs!" Miradyn beams.

"Oh, *did* you, now?" Myrval looks between the kittens, lifting of all three of their eyebrows teasingly. "I could have sworn I gave the three of you enough reading to keep you busy until this evening."

"We worked together to finish it!" Melbryl giggles.

"Can we go play outside in the shiny white stuff now?" asks Miradyn before either adult can question the point of their lessons further. They reach up and readjust their bow with their upper hands.

Myrval and Taimri share a look. There's no question they'll need to check just how "done" the lesson packs really are later. It's not that the kittens don't like learning or doing their schoolwork, really, but they're at an age to be easily distracted from it. The lodge offers quite a lot of distractions for curious kittens, too.

After a moment, Taimri chuckles. "It's called 'snow,' Mirseni, I *know* I've told you that," she says, clucking her tongue affectionately. She has little nicknames for all three of the kittens, just like she does for Myrval. "And you're hardly dressed to go out in it, yes?"

"We were waiting for you, Äiti!" Miradyn giggles again and makes a sweeping gesture to their two littermates. "But we already put our sweaters on! We even found one of Entile River's sweaters for Mer to wear over theirs so they won't get chilled again."

"Yes, we can see that," Myrval interjects, thoroughly amused but doing their best to keep a serious tone. "But your mother *is* right—you have your ears uncovered and you'll need to find your coats and snow-pants and boots too, if you don't want to freeze out there. The courtyard here is kept warm for us, remember? That's what the atmosphere shield up there is for. Outside is much colder." Myrval gestures up at the shimmering not-a-roof between themself and the sky. After a moment, they tilt their head to one side, twitching an ear curiously. "Why in the *stars* do you want to go out in the snow again, anyway?"

"Because it's *shiny*!" Melbryl giggles, then shifts to a more matter-of-fact tone. "But mostly because Mer hasn't gotten to come with us when Äiti's taken us out to explore since the day we got here—and we *promised* we'd take them out to play too today, now that they're not planet-sick anymore."

The two Rangers share another look. They're both keenly aware of how small and somewhat fragile little Merlani still is as a 'survivor-smallest' kitten. Even though they finally seem to be starting to catch up with their littermates physically, and *mentally* there's never been a difference between the three, Merlani is just over half the size a seven-year-old Florivan should be. Such kittens are relatively uncommon, as it's something of a miracle for one to live long enough for their eyes to open—much less to grow to adulthood the way Myrval themself has.

The bout of 'planet-sickness,' as the kittens call it, had really been Merlani's having become badly chilled on the day the family arrived at the lodge. As a result, they'd been ill and in and out of a torpor state for the better part of a week. Thankfully, Merlani seems to have made a full recovery now—not that this keeps anyone from worrying about them.

Myrval can't help worrying a bit more about their smallest nibling in general than they do about Miradyn and Melbryl, if only because they *remember* what it was like to grow up smaller and physically weaker than their littermate. Those memories also tell them, though, that worry can't be allowed too much priority where growing kittens are concerned. All three of the kittens remind them so much of Marbree, too, that they know forbidding the any of them from going out would only encourage a well-meaning and potentially disastrous escape.

"Well," Myrval says at last, "we have a *lot* of bundling up to do if you think I'm going to let all three of you go out." They sigh dramatically and wade over to the side of the spring pool where their robe and the neatly-folded pile of towels are sitting.

"Thank you, Entile River!" chorus the kittens, pouncing Myrval with a hug as soon as they're out of the water.

"Ack! Kittens! Let me dry off first, will you?"

Taimri also makes her way over to the towels, not even trying to hold back her laughter at the sight anymore.

★

ELSEWHERE IN THE SAME MOUNTAIN RANGE, A group of fifteen somewhat frazzled young pilots are attempting to find their way through a snow-covered forest. Each of them is dressed in the same sort of Academy-issue snowsuit: light grey, with the Tactical Flight department's yellow accents at the cuffs and collars and the cadet's surname on the back of their jacket over the ACNW Academy crest. A few of them sport additional colors signifying their cross-training in other departments.

Were they in an ordinary forest on Earth in such conditions as these, with a thick blanket of snow covering most of the ground and dusting the surfaces of the large boulders which are scattered among the trees, the cadets might easily blend in to the scenery. This forest, though, is made up of Hideaway's native plants. The bark of the trees around them is all in shades of pink or red, and the evergreen shrubs near their bases are covered in sharp turquoise-green needles. The cadets have been fortunate not to lose track of each other for very long, thanks to that.

At the moment, the three most senior cadets are standing at the bank of a small river and discussing their options for crossing it, while most of the others are taking a few moments to rest. The final two members of the group, both first-year students, are just now coming out of the thicker part of the forest to join their classmates. With them is their instructor, a slightly shorter-than-average gentleman whose dark beard is beginning to go salt-and-pepper at his temples and is currently quite a bit scruffier than he usually keeps it. Unlike the cadets, his snowsuit is charcoal grey save for the jacket, which is Defense Fleet-issue ivory and bears his old squadron's insignia instead of the Academy's. Over this figure of a horse rearing, the name "Barker" is printed in bold emerald green.

This is none other than George Barker, the man Ocean Marbrec's kittens call their father. He's having a far better afternoon than his cadets are, but that's a bit of the point of this exercise. His blue eyes sparkle with held-in laughter as he leans just a little more heavily on the shoulder of the cadet who's currently in charge of helping him walk. "I *do* hope it's not too much farther, Mr. Noble," he says, drawling out the words in an exaggerated impersonation of a certain snooty protocol officer he used to know, "you poor young things just might have to carry me if these blasted hills get any steeper."

Cadet Noble sets his free hand over his face for a moment to cover whatever expression he was about to make, then pauses to shake a few stray snowflakes off of the glove. "Well, sir... We'll have to ask one of the upperclassmen about that."

On George's other side, Cadet Ionescu stifles a laugh. "Of course we will, *Mr. Ambassador*," she says, pitching her voice louder now. "Our upperclassmen are much stronger than the two of us, you know. I'm sure they'd be *delighted* to do any carrying you need today."

George nods sagely, although he's finding it hard to keep a straight face. These two have been good sports about their assigned task for the survival trip, that's for sure. He may be there to supervise things and ultimately make sure his cadets learn how to handle whatever environment they might need to make an emergency landing into, but getting to play the part of the injured dignitary the lot of them have to keep alive is a guilty pleasure of his. He gets to know the newest members of the cohort best this way, since they're always the ones the group assigns to look after their "troublesome passenger."

From the low boulder where he and the other second and third year cadets are sitting, Cadet Gravener calls back towards Ionescu without turning to look up from the map he's been reading. The extra set of blue departmental stripes on his sleeves and collar make him unmistakable, even when one can't see the name written on his back. "Don't even think about asking me, Maria—Abalone and I got stuck doing that the *last* time I was on one of these."

"Now, now, Mr. Gravener..." George does his best mock-hobble over to the boulder, still playing up his injured ambassador persona. "Wouldn't that *delightful* counterpart of yours expect you to be more respectful towards your elders? Great Scott, boy, don't you know who I *am*?" He makes a point of sputtering the last word.

Gravener turns his head now, and with a raised eyebrow and a deadpan tone replies, "Sir, at the moment I'm not all that sure *you* know who you are."

George can't help laughing at that, and neither can the rest of the group. He dusts off a patch of the large, roughly flat boulder his cadets have chosen for a resting place and takes a seat, letting the persona drop. "Okay, point to you, Gravener. You got me there."

"How many more points do we need to be rid of the Ambassador altogether, sir?" Noble shrugs his backpack off and stretches, pausing here and there to dust a bit of snow off of himself.

"Oh..." George shrugs, looking up at the clouds through the bare pink branches of the canopy for a few moments. "I'll let you know when you have enough. Your goal is to keep the fool alive, mind."

"He's not all that good at keeping *himself* alive, though, is he?" Ionescu quips.

"And that's why you lot need practice keeping that sort of fellow safe, yes." George shakes his head. "Believe it or not, the real ones are worse than I could ever pretend to be, some of them."

"Really, sir?" Cadet Kirsch, one of the three seniors, calls down from the tall, sturdy tree form of the evergreen plant they're now climbing, presumably to get a better view of the landscape on the other side of the river. "You say that every year, but I still can hardly believe it."

"Just wait 'till you start ferrying folks around, Kirsch," George calls back, "I've met a few in my day that can try the patience of a saint—or a Florivan, for that matter." He pauses, shaking his head at an errant memory of the time he and Breezy were the ones on an all-too-real survival trek like this with a particularly prickly set of passengers who were not only angry and frightened by the situation, but also happened to loathe each other. That was the first time he'd ever witnessed his counterpart genuinely lose their temper, too. Something about being cussed out by a person whose species was legendary for being mild-mannered, helpful pacifists had a way of making folks decide to get along, at least for a little while.

"If you say so, sir." Kirsch disappears up into the snow-covered branches.

"I do—and mind your step coming down from there, Kirsch! I'll never hear the end of it if one of you gets injured before we make it to the lodge."

"No," says Gravener, offering George a steaming cup from the thermos of coffee the cadets are passing around, "I don't think Storm would be too happy about that."

George accepts the liquid warmth happily. Snowy treks like this *require* coffee—although he can't say much for the quality of coffee his young pilots have been able to brew over their morning campfires.

"Oh, they wouldn't. I've no doubt they're still disappointed River wouldn't let them come along to be our field medic... but they're far more forgiving than the folks up at Academy Medical are." He takes a sip from the cup and grimaces lightly at the bitterness before adding, "and we both know that Abalone wants *you* returned in one piece, so don't go falling into any holes again because you're not watching where you're going."

"Sir, I only did that once..." Gravener protests, then glances to the two first-year cadets with a grin. "Besides, I only missed seeing the hole because I was trying to keep a certain over-acting 'ambassador' upright and walking forward after he 'just needed to rest for a minute' and then the next thing I knew we were an hour behind the rest of the group."

George stifles a laugh. "All the more reason you should have been paying attention—you'd have saved the rest of the Nav/Quan cohort from having to deal with both of us being genuinely injured." He'll freely admit that this particular young man is a favorite student of his, in no small part due to the hours the two of them had spent in said hole waiting for Gravener's Florivan counterpart to catch up to the other students and the Nav/Quan department's lead instructors and then bring help back to get them out.

"Note to self," says Ionescu, leaning over to stage whisper to Noble, "watch where we're walking, or he'll find an excuse to fall on us..."

George is about to say something witty in response, but Kirsch's flurry of a descent from the tree distracts him. Aside from the miniature blizzard falling as they brush past branches on the way down, Kirsch practically leaps the last few feet and lands with a soft thud in the deep snowdrift at the tree's base. The cadet seems startled, which is never a good sign on one of these hikes. "Something after you, Cadet?"

"Ah, well, yes sir?" Kirsch stands and dusts most of the snow off themself, then stares up into the tree. "Or no, I guess. I don't see it now."

George comes over and looks up into the now-snowless clusters of sharp turquoise foliage that line the tree's salmon-pink branches. "And just what was 'it', then?"

"I don't know, sir. I thought there was some sort of... sparkly little thing flying around my head, while I was in the upper branches."

"Sparkly little thing," George repeats, raising an eyebrow. He's familiar with all of the native wildlife he should be expecting his cadets to encounter in this forest. That description doesn't match any of them.

"It was probably just a trick of the light on the snow," Kirsch says, reaching up to take off their hat and shake it free of snow.

"Probably," George agrees. "But if you see it again, let me know." He walks with Kirsch over to where the other two senior cadets are waiting. "Now, how do you three figure on leading us across this river?"

"Well, sir," Kirsch begins, still sounding a touch flustered, "it looked like there's a natural crossing just downstream of here where there's boulders we could hop between..."

"Or," says Cadet Kells, crossing her arms lightly, "we follow the map and divert upstream about a kilometer to use the trail bridge. That way, I don't have to treat anyone for hypothermia or head injuries because they slipped on an icy rock." Kells one of George's best pilots, but she's also working on her Field Medicine certificate. That no-nonsense tone of hers unmistakably belongs to someone who's been on far too many of these survival training excursions to think her first aid skills won't be needed by the end of it.

George nods. "Good, good, you have options! Now, considering that you have an 'injured' person with you, what are you going to do?"

The third of the seniors, Cadet Halpern, groans. "Sir, do you *have* to be injured while we're crossing the river?"

"It's part of the exercise, Halpern," George replies. "Don't worry, I'll try not to be too hard on you regardless of what route you pick—I'm not keen on going swimming myself today, you know..."

“ALL RIGHT, NOW, THAT SHOULD BE ALL OF YOU properly dressed! What do you think, River?”

“I *think* all four of you would be better off staying here in the lodge where it’s warm.” Myrval smirks pointedly at their counterpart as they inspect their niblings again.

Each of the kittens has been kitted out with several layers of clothing: thermal undergarments, shirt, sweater, trousers, quilted snowsuit jacket, matching snowsuit pants, two pairs of socks, and snow-boots. The kittens’ long prehensile tails have each been carefully tucked down one pant leg to protect them from frostbite, and each of their four-fingered hands has been encased in both a thermal lining glove and a thick fleece-lined mitten. On top of all of this, each kitten has a wide, plush scarf wrapped around their neck and a loose-fitting pompom-topped hat that completely covers their large catlike ears.

On little Merlani, all of this protective warm layering makes them look like something of a yellow marshmallow with four arms and a pair of equally marshmallow-shaped legs. Only their three golden eyes are visible. The other two kittens are just enough taller that the layers look less comical and allow them a greater range of motion.

Myrval nods approvingly. "Considering that if we bundle the three of you up any more, you won't be able to walk... I'll call this acceptable."

Taimri chuckles and readjusts her own lighter-weight snow jacket. Although she's not in as many layers as the kittens, she still has a purple, pink, and yellow striped version of the same sort of pompom-topped hat and matching gloves and scarf to protect her from the cold. "No need to worry, River, we'll come in as soon as anyone starts feeling cold, yes? Now..." She motions for the kittens to come over to the bench beside the lodge's wide front window with her. "Why don't we send George a picture of this while everyone is still cooperating about being bundled up?"

Myrval pulls out their pocket-com and takes the photo, and then several more for good measure, all the while shaking their head in amusement at the seemingly universal parental affectation of wanting pictures of their offspring to show to people. They have to admit, though, that their counterpart and their niblings are absolutely adorable all dressed up for their snow excursion.

As they document the moment, Myrval is struck with a fond, albeit sadness-tinged, memory of their *own* parent's collection of printed and carefully assembled albums filled with images of all their many older siblings and extended or chosen family members. In their childhood, that collection had taken up an entire floor-to-ceiling bookcase in their family's home in the Procyon Sanctuary. Now, all that's left of it are the portions contained in the volumes their parent had given Myrval and Marbree to keep with them when they'd left home for their apprenticeship and the ones that their handful of star-jumping older siblings carried. Between the War and the losses that time has brought since, all but one of the surviving volumes sit together on a shelf in Myrval's quarters aboard *Atascosa*. A matching, updated copy has been made for each of these three kittens who are Myrval's only remaining blood-kin.

Between George and Taimri's efforts, though, by now the whole extended family has an extensive collection of pictures of the kittens growing up. Myrval's printed albums dedicated to thir sweet little niblings take up a whole shelf in themselves.

The kittens pose happily for the photos with their mother, Melbryl in purple and Miradyn in pink on either side of her and little Merlani-the-yellow-marshmallow sitting in her lap. Taimri's multicolored accessories match the kittens perfectly. They couldn't look more clearly *hers*, in Myrval's opinion, even if the kittens had been willing to pick a single color of snow gear. They've tried before to explain to the kittens that traditionally, they'd all wear the colors of their household's Elder, but George had gotten the three of them into the habit of being color-coded so folks at the AC-NW space station could tell them apart when they were all still small silver-furred things.

Rather, he'd color-coded the kittens with neatly tied bows around their middles for a family portrait *once*, and little Miradyn had been so taken with the concept that they've insisted on being "the one with the pink bow" ever since. The other two aren't all that concerned with the color of their clothing, so long as it's different from each other, but if given a choice in the matter, Miradyn will invariably be in as many shades of pink as they can manage to fit into one outfit. *Frilly* pink at that, for preference.

Much to Myrval's lightly frustrated amusement, their littermate's offspring are entirely too fond of being individually distinguished to be persuaded to wear family colors for anything other than formal occasions, even though they're old enough now that even humans who aren't familiar with Florivans can tell them apart with a glance. Then again, in the current case, letting them be brightly colored like this is probably for the best. Even with the touches of amber Myrval and the kittens wear in their traditional Florivan-style clothes now that they belong to Elder Celadon's household, their main color is still in honor of Myrval's parent—and *white* snow-suits would hardly have been practical.

"You're sure you don't want to come with us, Jokeni?" Taimri teases while she's inspecting the pictures and choosing the best one to forward to her husband.

"Oh, no. I'll be right here by the fire where it's *warm*, thank you very much." Myrval laughs and gestures out through the large window at the snow-covered hillside. "I'll make sure to sit where I can see you out there in case you need me." They're content with watching this time, even though they treasure every chance they get to play with their family. Their recently-injured leg doesn't care for the cold at all, and they're in too good a mood to encourage those residual nerve twinges to return.

"All right, then." Taimri picks Merlani up and waves to the other two to follow her. "Come on, kittens! We should go make our escape before your entile changes their mind about letting us, yes?"

"Yes, Äiti!" Melbryl and Miradyn happily scamper behind her out the front door and into the snow.

Myrval acquires a pot of mint tea for themself and a thick-woven tartan lap blanket and settles into one of the large plush armchairs beside the window to watch their family playing in the snow. Contented as they are at the moment, Myrval can't help but think about how *pleased* their littermate would have been with how these kittens of theirs are turning out—and that, bittersweet as the thought is, Marbree would have been right out there in the snow with the rest of them causing chaos.

You'd be out there, all right, Marbree... and Nida too, I'm sure. Myrval muses, sipping their tea slowly. *And probably Sky and Stream. You were all the adventurous sort.* They'd had a whole host of other older siblings too, of course, but they'd never met any of them. Their home planet's legendary Periodic Jungle Plagues had seen to that. Still, Myrval is certain that all of them would have been delighted to play in the snow with Marbree's kittens. Their parent's streak of adventuresome trouble-making tendencies had passed down to just about all of their offspring. Only Myrval themself and little Merlani hadn't seemed to inherit it to the same extent.

Well... Myrval corrects themself after pausing to take a picture through the window of the kittens' antics out in the snow with their counterpart, *Merlani, at least. I did wind up a Ranger, after all. But it's not like I'm the one who causes any of the adventure that finds me...*

They'd never admit to enjoying it, either. Myrval's always been stubborn about maintaining their image as the sensible member of the family.

They smile softly at the memories and then send the additional pictures on to George too, adding an appropriate note:

```
Tam's having more fun out in the
snow than you are, I expect. If
you decided you're ready to be
rescued, you'll have to wait until
the kittens bring her back. I'm not
about to be the one going out into
this frigid nonsense to pick you up.
```

Within a few minutes, they hear the light chime signaling that he's responded. It's one of the distinctive sounds that lets them know immediately which person's sent the message, but like all of their alert tones, it's set to be inaudible to human ears. Myrval's never been the sort to disrupt the people around them with their communications, after all, and as a Ranger, being more discrete about matters comes in handy more often than not.

Their ears twitch with amusement when they read the reply. It's easy to hear George's distinctive inflections in their mind as they do.

```
What, River, you're not out teaching
them to throw snowballs? Here I'd
```

He's attached a picture of his band of young pilots posing dramatically in front of one of the larger and more colorful thermal pools that dotted the landscape. They recognize the spot; there's a rather large print of a photograph of it hanging over the sofa in their family's suite here at the lodge. Despite the steam coming up off of the water behind them, all Myrval can think looking at the collection of human faces is that the poor things look like they must be *cold*.

They can only imagine how unpleasant hiking through the wilderness for so long in this sort of weather must be, even if the landscape is admittedly beautiful. They say as much in their reply:

```
wind   up   wounded   or   frostbitten
because   you've   pushed   them   too
far,   it's   your   own   fault.   Don't
let  it  happen.  I'm  not  interested
in  listening  to  Storm  scolding  and
fussing  over  you  all  the  way  back
to  ACNW  because  you  went  and  did
something  truly  foolish.

I'd  expect  Tam  wants  you  to  arrive
intact,  too.
```

Myrval pauses after they've sent the message, and then adds one final postscript before they set their pocket-com up on the armrest of their chair to record a little video of the kittens playing with Taimri to send to the rest of their family. The scene is too adorable not to share, with Miradyn and Melbryl scampering all over the place trying to roll up a big lump of snow for whatever reason and little Merlani waddling along and occasionally tossing some of the snow up into the air and then staring in wonder as it falls back down.

Not that they'd ever admit it out loud, but Myrval does, deep down, think it all looks like fun. Entirely too cold to participate in themself, but fun.

Yes, Marbree, they think, tucking the blanket around themself a little closer even though the lodge is reasonably warm, *your kittens are taking after you and Nida in the best ways. I can't say much for their choice of places to play, but they can find an adventure to make out of just about anywhere...*

★

GEORGE LAUGHS OUT LOUD WHEN HE READS THE final message from his adoptive sibling.

```
I'd take that bet, by the way, but
I don't want to give the universe
an excuse to get you into trouble
just to spite me.

See to it that you win.
```

River's sense of humor is so dry he sometimes wonders how it belongs to a Florivan. Their barbs have grown far more affectionate over the years, though. It might not be explicit, but it's clear to him that they're just as concerned with his well-being as anyone.

Maybe more, even, he thinks to himself. River has struck him as a bit of a worrier from the moment they met. Ever since losing Breezy, they've been subtly paranoid about the health and safety of the remainder of the family. George had been rather surprised when he finally realized that this extended to him, too.

"...Something amusing, sir?" Cadet Ionescu looks at him with no shortage of suspicion in her expression. She's taking her turn at being the one to guide and support the group's supposedly injured person.

George tucks his pocket-com back into the depths of his snowsuit's pockets, not bothering to stifle the grin on his own face. "You could say that. Don't worry, it's not any devious plan sort of thing."

On his other side, he catches a glimpse of Cadet Noble shaking his head somberly. Noble doesn't say anything to go with the gesture, though.

"Well, then..." Ionescu continues staring at him warily for a few moments, then brightens. "If it's not any business of the *Ambassador's*, then that's all right."

"Trust me, it's not." George finds himself chuckling again. "River doesn't put up with him."

"Having met Captain River," says Noble, now holding a low-hanging branch across the path made by the rest of the group out of the way so George and Ionescu can pass, "I would expect not."

Ionescu seems to finish the thought for him. "They probably have to put up with too many *real* folks like him to tolerate your impressions, huh?"

"That about sums it up." George agrees. Shifting his posture and tone of voice, he picks up the character he's supposed to be playing again. "Now, you two aren't going to let us get any further behind the group, are you? I won't stand for being left behind to freeze!"

"No, sir," says Noble. "We've almost caught up to them."

"They wouldn't dare leave us behind," Ionescu adds. "Besides, they're not exactly being stealthy about walking in this snow."

"No," says Noble. "Leaving a nice clear path for us, even."

George has decided by now that this pair of first years balance each other far more nicely than he'd expected. He's looking forward to seeing what they'll be able to accomplish once they've passed their current semester of basic flight training and can be put into Darter simulations. His impression is that they'll take to flying in tandem splendidly. There's a certain amount of instinctive personality compatibility required for that; one has to be comfortable enough with the other pilot to almost feel where they're moving before they get there, regardless of which one is taking lead. Noble and Ionescu already seem to be developing that sort of unspoken understanding.

As if in example of his thoughts, he catches a glimpse of a small jerk to one side of Noble's head. Without even commenting on it, Ionescu steers George in that direction just enough to avoid both of them tripping on a large rock that's been exposed by all of the other cadets disturbing the snow in front of them.

George considers it thoughtfully as they continue onwards. *Yes, these two as half of a squadron's wing would be excellent...*

In the back of his mind, there's a melody circulating. It's one of the many songs old Brother Hubert had about ancient sailing ships, hardworking men of ages past, and faraway oceans that have filled up any bit of spare room available in George's consciousness for as long as he can remember. Breezy had always been fond of his mental catalog of shanties and folk songs; Colonel Vasquez and the rest of the Mustangs had vaguely tolerated them. That had all been such a long time ago.

As his life stands now, he's pretty lucky. The kittens love the old songs just as much as he had as a child, thankfully. Taimri does too, and one of these days he's going to figure out how to properly pronounce the words to the songs she'd brought into their marriage so that he can sing them instead of just getting them stuck in his head for days. River makes a show of being vaguely annoyed by George's singing, but he's known for a while now that they genuinely enjoy it. On the occasions they can be persuaded to join in, River has a fine voice of their own, too.

There's a sudden gust of wind across the path, sending a flurry of snowflakes into the air as it swirls through the alien forest. George looks up at the sky thoughtfully. The clouds don't seem too threatening, at least. They're all some ways off in the distance over the next mountain.

Still, the weather has that old song swirling through his thoughts.

For there blow some cold nor'westers on the banks of Newfoundland...

"Um... sir?" Noble's voice cuts in over the melody of memories.

George turns to look at him, waiting for the actual question.

Noble hesitates, then asks, "do Ambassadors generally hum, or is that just you?"

"Oh, I'd wager some do." George shrugs lightly, having not been aware that he *was* humming. It's hardly the first time that's happened, though. The music tends to find its way out of him when his mind has a chance to wander.

Before Noble can press the question, Ionescu stops walking and whirls around, as if trying to keep her eyes on something. "Did either of you see that?"

"See what?" Noble turns to look in the same direction.

So does George, dropping what was left of his persona. When cadets start seeing things, it's definitely time to give them a break from their imaginary charges. "I didn't see anything either. What did you see, Ionescu?"

"It was... oh, a little sparkly thing like a firefly or something. Kind of green?" Ionescu rubs at her eyes. "I could have sworn it flew up from behind me after that big gust shook all the trees and was sort of fluttering around us until you two started talking again."

"Probably just a bit of snow catching the light," says Noble.

"Probably," George agrees. "Staring at all the whiteness can do odd things to the eyes—same as staring out into the galaxy can do while you're flying." He's no stranger to that effect, that's for sure. Then again, he's also seen a lot of things most folks wouldn't believe could be real, too.

"Ah. Probably so, sir." Ionescu nods and starts walking again.

George and Noble fall into step with her.

"Still," he says, after a few moments, "if you see it again, give us a nudge before it flies away. I'd like to see what sort of firefly could survive in this snow."

"Yes, sir." Ionescu glances behind her one last time, then turns her attention back to George. "So, sir, what song was that? I don't think I've heard it."

"Well, now!" George chuckles. It's not often he gets a perfect opening to pass on one of his songs. It's well worth dropping all pretense of being injured or irritating, for sure. "It's an old one from Earth about sailing to a frozen shore..."

★

OCEAN MERLANI'S FIRST IMPRESSION OF SNOW
upon their arrival at the lodge had been that the
shiny white stuff was *entirely* too cold and that they would
much rather stay safely cuddled indoors under a blanket
with their entile instead of out running around in it.

After having been ill and cooped up in the lodge
for days and not being allowed to do much of anything,
though, *any* form of fun with their littermates is appealing.
Now that they're feeling better, Merlani has decided to
give the snow a second chance. Their littermates, after all,
have assured them that playing in the snow is fun enough
to make it worth being outside in the cold.

Merlani has never liked having to be left out of fun
things just because they're smaller and more sensitive—not
that Mir and Mel would ever intentionally leave them out.

What Merlani finds now, after their mother sets them down so she can have her hands free to help them all build a 'snow-person' like she used to do when she was a child on Earth, is that snow is *still* cold and somewhat wet, but also *sparkly* and fun to toss up into the air so they can watch all of the pretty water crystals fall back down. It reminds them of some of the mineral specimens in the Geology Department's collection back at their home on the ACNW space station, with the way the light glitters off of the individual bits of ice, but far softer.

They'd never seen snow for themself before coming here. The space station where they live doesn't exactly *have* weather. Merlani's always been fascinated by stories about it, though. Most of Äiti's weather stories from when she was little are about snow. Entile River's are about jungle rains, when they're willing to talk about their home at all. Dad only has weather stories from places he's visited, since he's always lived on starships and space stations.

When Merlani tries to run after their littermates to find stones to use for facial features on the vaguely person-shaped pile of snow the four of them have been assembling, they discover that snow can be *deceptively* unstable to walk on. One moment, they're clambering over a snowdrift; the next, they find themself all but submerged.

It's *cold* inside the snow.

Their lower two eyes can only see sparkling, chilly whiteness. Their third eye is just above the surface of the snow, looking out over the smooth footprint-marked expanse. Their littermates are still scampering towards the forest. They haven't noticed yet that Merlani is no longer shuffling along behind them.

Within a couple of moments, Äiti appears to help Merlani dig themself out. They do need help, too, because the snowdrift is *deep* and the layers and layers of clothes they're wearing makes it hard to move all four of their arms with any coordination. They're distinctly aware of how unhelpful their usually-useful prehensile tail is when it's imprisioned down a trouser leg, too.

"Oh, dear," says Äiti through giggles as she's pulling Merlani up out of the snow hole. "Merlakka, are you all right? You didn't hurt yourself when you fell?"

She's speaking in her ancestral language instead of Human Standard, like she usually does when it's just her and Merlani and their littermates. Äiti told them once that it was her job to pass things like that down to them, just like it would have been if she'd ever decided to have human children. It's part of what makes having her as one of their parents *special*.

"I'm okay, Äiti," Merlani replies, a bit embarrassed. "The snow tried to eat me!"

"Snow does that sometimes." Äiti kneels to be closer to their height and starts dusting the snow off of them. "Perhaps I should find you some *lumikengät* before we come out to do this again."

"*Lumikengät* is 'snowshoes' in Standard, right?" Merlani doesn't recognize the new word, even though they're fluent enough to know that it's made of '*lumi*,' which is the stuff they've been playing in, and '*kenkiä*' for shoes.

"It is!" Äiti is still in the middle of re-wrapping Merlani's now-snow-free scarf around them. "Remind me when we get in for the night and I'll pull up some pictures to show you."

Merlani nods, although with all of the layers they're wearing, they're not sure if she can see it. "Do snowshoes keep the snow from eating you, Äiti?"

"Yes, that's what they're for, in a way." Their mother giggles again and stands. She pauses a moment to dust the snow off of her own legs and then picks Merlani up. "Come on, let's catch up to Miradyn and Melbryl before they get lost out here, yes?"

In the time it's taken for their mother to find them a way out of the snow-hole, their littermates have gone far enough into the alien trees that even Merlani's keen ears can only barely hear the sounds of them laughing—although that might be because their nice warm hat muffles a portion of the things they would normally be able to hear. Luckily, Mir and Mel have left a clear trail of footprints in the snow for Äiti to follow.

Merlani nods and makes themself comfortable hanging on to her. They're not always content with being the smallest, but they do appreciate being small enough still to be carried. It reminds them of when they were a much smaller silver-furred kitten and could ride everywhere in the warm safety of someone's pockets.

"So, are you having fun, Merlakka?"

"Mm..." Merlani thinks about it for a moment before nuzzling their face a little closer into her neck to absorb some of the extra warmth from her scarf. "Yes? Except for the snow eating me. And it's *cold*."

Äiti laughs and reaches up to ruffle their ears through the hat. "You sound just like your entile. Once we catch your siblings, we'll all go in and have tea and snacks so you can thaw out. That sounds good, yes?"

"Yes, please." Merlani's eyes catch something bright pink standing out from all the whiteness off to the side over Äiti's shoulder. They point towards it before she can walk past. "Äiti? What's that?"

"I *do* believe it's one of Miradyn's mittens," says Äiti, clucking her tongue. She goes over and picks it up, handing it to Merlani. "Here, hold this for me until we can return it to them, yes? I can't see why they'd have taken it off... I *know* I reminded them they need to wear both sets of hand-covers to keep their fingers warm."

Merlani shrugs, also unable to think of a reason why Mir would have discarded the soft warm thing. They're rather fond of their own mittens and being able to feel their fingers, themself.

A few moments later, Merlani's ears prick up under their hat, not at the presence of a sound but at the *absence* of one.

"Äiti?" Merlani asks, looking around them and down towards the trail of small footprints in the snow.

"Yes, Merlakka? What is it?"

"Can I take my hat off?"

"What? Why? I know it's a bit bulky, but it's there to keep your ears from getting frostbitten, yes?"

"No, it's not that—I like it, actually—but I can't hear Mir and Mel anymore."

"Oh?" A momentary look of concern flashes over Äiti's face before she brightens back to her usual cheerful person-who-always-knows-what-to-do expression. "Yes, then, but just for a minute or two. When your ears start to get cold, you'll put it back on, yes?"

"Yes, Äiti." Merlani carefully pulls their hat back to let their large catlike ears out and swivels them around to try to pinpoint the familiar sounds of their littermates.

Äiti, in the meantime, continues following the trail Mir and Mel have left through the forest. She comes to a place where a great boulder and outcropping of stones have sheltered the ground from the piling up of the snow. A wide cave next to the boulder leads through to the other side of the mountain. It seems like a reinforced tunnel, though, with metal supports in place periodically along the length of it as can be seen from the opening and lights suspended at regular intervals between them.

"Oh, dear." Äiti sets Merlani down for a moment and pulls out her pocket com. "I know I told those two not to go too far... Can you hear them now, Merlakka?"

Merlani quiets themself and focuses with their eyes closed on all of the sounds around them.

Wind.

One of the small alien forest creatures digging in the ground under the snow.

Drips of water deep in the tunnel.

And... there!

Merlani opens their eyes and pulls their hat back on so their ears can warm up again.

"I can, now!" They point into the tunnel with one of their upper hands. "They're somewhere in there, almost to the other side."

Äiti clucks her tongue again. "Your entile is *not* going to be happy about this. Let me send them a message to say where we're going and then you and I will go find your littermates, yes?"

Since there's no snow inside the tunnel, Merlani doesn't have to worry about getting swallowed by it again. As soon as Äiti is done sending messages, Merlani reaches up and takes her hand with one of their upper ones so they can hold it while they walk. Even through both their mittens and her gloves, they can still feel a bit of reassuring warmth.

★

MYRVAL'S PLEASANT AFTERNOON SITTING BY the fire is interrupted by a ping from their counterpart, not long after they'd seen her and the kittens scampering off beyond the edge of what they can see through the front windows of the lodge's common area.

```
Kittens  scampered  a  bit  too  far.
They're somewhere on the other side
of  that  tunnel  that  leads  through
to  the  back  of  the  ridge. Mer and I
are going through to get them.
```

Myrval sighs and twitches an ear in mild exasperation while they tap back a reply.

```
Is  Mer  okay  going  with  you? I can
meet  you  halfway  if  you  want  to
send them back first.
```

A few moments later, they receive another ping from Taimri:

> They're good. I'd wager it'd take longer for you to meet us by now than for us to grab Mir and Mel and come back. I'll let you know if anything changes.

> Looks like no reception in the tunnel, I'll check in with you on the other side.

As Myrval is tapping out an acknowledgment of this, two things interrupt them one after the other. The first is a bright-colored local weather alert flashing across the holoscreen, announcing that a rather severe blizzard is on its way to the mountains surrounding the lodge and should be arriving within four or five hours. The second interruption is one of the staff members from the lodge approaching them, right when they're in the middle of changing the text of their message to make sure Taimri will be *aware* of the blizzard in case she hasn't seen the alert herself.

"Excuse me, Captain River," says the old human politely, leaning on his cane. "I know that you and your counterpart are here on vacation, but we've been alerted to some dangerous weather conditions…"

"I'm aware, the alert just came through—just a moment." Myrval quickly sends the message telling Taimri to get in touch with them as soon as she has reception again and then turns all three eyes up to the lodge's caretaker. "Now, how can I help you?"

The caretaker doesn't waste any time getting to the point. "I've sent out copies of the alert to all of the hiking groups and researchers in the area to let them know that they'll need to return here for shelter before the storm arrives. From the look of the forecast, it won't be safe for anyone to remain at their campsites. I've already dispatched the staff members I can spare to collect the majority of the people registered as camping in the more distant parts of the lodge's jurisdiction... but considering how quickly this storm has developed, I'd appreciate having some help to retrieve the rest of our guests. There's a few folks we haven't confirmed contact with recently who we might not locate in time otherwise."

Myrval nods. "All right, then. If you can get me a list of names and estimated coordinates together while I get my coats on, I'll pick Tam up on the way and we'll bring them all in for you. Do you have anyone fetching the AC-NW flight cadet bunch yet?"

"Yes, they're on the list of folks I need you to bring in. I expected you'd want to, since you dropped them off and all." The old man gives Myrval a bit of a wave as he turns to go. "I have a snow-flitter warming up for you on the landing pad. Glad you're here to help, Ranger."

Myrval sends another ping to Taimri to let her know what's going on and then scurries off to their guest room to change into warmer clothes. They can't help but think that if Marbree was here to see this, they'd be *highly* amused that Myrval has, once again and despite their best efforts, failed to stay out of the snow.

★

"**Ä**ITI! THAT'S ANOTHER ONE OF MEL'S MITTENS!" Merlani scurries over to a little alcove in the side of the tunnel's far end. They pick up the bright purple thing that's caught their eyes. "And it's *wet*, for some reason?"

"That'll be the snow melting on it... I still don't see a reason for the two of them to shed these." Äiti shakes her head. "Remind me that I need to give them the frostbite lecture again when we find them, will you?"

"Yes, Äiti." Merlani tucks the purple mitten into their coat's pockets with the other three they're already carrying, making a matched pair of each color. Their own hands are starting to get cold even through the yellow mittens they're wearing and the liner gloves underneath, so they don't know how their littermates are managing with at least one pair of hands each more exposed to the chilly air.

A bright series of pinging sounds echo out of Äiti's jacket as the two of them come out of the tunnel and into the clear, sheltered area on the other side. She pulls out her pocket-com and flicks through the messages for a few moments before clucking her tongue again and typing something back.

"Is something wrong, Äiti?" Merlani looks up at her curiously.

"Oh, no, just a bit of bad weather heading this way." Äiti tucks the little device back into the pocket it lives in. "Your entile is going to come in one of the lodge's flitters and pick the four of us up once we've found Mir and Mel— and then we have a few people to find and take back to the lodge with us. A bit of an extra adventure today, yes?" She smiles in a bright, reassuring way and points to a pair of footprint trails heading through the snow and down the hillside. "It looks like they went that way."

As the two of them follow the footprints, the incline is steep enough and the snow deep enough that after three or four steps, Merlani has to be picked up and carried again. With all of their bulky snow clothes on, they can't keep up with Äiti's long legs without risking tumbling down the hill.

Large fluffy flakes of new snow begin to drift down from the growing clouds in the sky as they walk. Merlani pulls their scarf down just long enough to catch one of the snowflakes on their tongue like Äiti's told them she used to do. The snowflake melts almost immediately, and doesn't taste of much of anything besides *cold*.

The trail leads down to the base of the hill and along the banks of a hot spring stream. Äiti has to carefully step between a series of large frost-covered stones in order to cross the steam-traced water so she can follow the rest of the trail from the other side deep into the forest. She has to carry Merlani all the way across, too, since their legs are too short and bundled-up to hop between the big rocks like their littermates must have.

It's not until the two of them have gotten far enough into this older growth of the alien trees that Merlani can only barely hear the sound of the water behind them that they pick up the sounds of their siblings' voices again.

"Äiti! I hear them! They're just up ahead."

"Finally! I was beginning to wonder if they'd be taking us all the way down out of the mountains to the other end of the continent, at this rate." Äiti only half-laughs this time—a sure sign that she's starting to get worried.

Merlani can understand why she would be. It's cold, after all, and their littermates have been gone on their adventure for a long time now. They're a little worried themself, but only a little. Their mother is there with them, and they know she'll find Mir and Mel soon. She always does. She's a *Ranger*. No one in the galaxy is better at hide-and-seek than her, except maybe Entile River.

A moment later, Merlani's ears prick up again. They're confused by what they hear, almost as much as they are by the odd not-quite-a-gust-of-wind sound that they've kept thinking they've heard since they entered this part of the alien forest. They take off their hat again to un-muffle their ears and focus better on the sound.

"There's another voice with them, Äiti," Merlani says, once they're sure of the sounds.

Äiti grows still, setting her free gloved hand around her ear to mimic the function of one of Merlani's far more sensitive ones so she can try to focus on the sounds herself.

"Do you recognize who it is, Merlakka?" she asks, her tone falling just a bit more serious. "We're too far away for me to hear them at all still."

Merlani closes their eyes and focuses all their attention on the sounds coming from the directions the footprints lead. "I don't know them, but they're human. Kinda like Dad, but a little higher-pitched and younger, I think?"

"Okay, then." Äiti starts walking again, albeit more slowly and in such a way that her footsteps on the snow are much less crunchy-sounding than before. "You keep listening, and tap on my shoulder if you hear any changes or if you recognize the voice. We're going to play a game with your littermates' new friend and be *quiet* so we can surprise them all when we find them, yes? I'll set you down when we get close enough that I can hear them." She has more of her usual conspiratorial cheerfulness back now, but still with that little current of serious hiding inside it that Merlani doesn't quiet understand.

Merlani nods anyway and continues listening.

A few minutes of slow walking later, Merlani starts to be able to hear words rather than just the tones of voices. It's mostly just Mir and Mel excitedly talking about snow and the snow-person they'd been building together, though, and how neat it is to be somewhere other than their home on the space station. All of that familiar chatter is interspersed with small comments and sounds of amusement from a middle-deep human voice which Merlani is now *certain* they've never met before. They've always been good at remembering voices and whose they are.

Soon, Äiti stops walking again and sets them down. She holds a finger to her lips as a sign for Merlani to stay quiet. This coincides with the human voice starting to talk again, asking Mir and Mel if they're cold.

There's a big boulder with one of the pink-barked variety of alien trees growing halfway on top of it between the place where Äiti stopped walking and the place where the voices are. From the other side of the boulder, Merlani hears their littermates talking to the human voice about the lodge and their entile and how they're all going to hopefully have tea once they get back to warm up.

Äiti listens to the voices with them for a few moments while she's fishing her pocket-com out of her jacket. She taps a few things on the holoscreen, then hands it to Merlani and gestures for them to stay put and wait while she goes to do the surprising.

Merlani nods and takes their place behind the boulder. They watch with interest as Äiti goes deeper into the trees to their right so she can quietly circle around to the front of it. Merlani doesn't remember *ever* seeing her get so interested in a game of impromptu hide-and-seek before. They suspect it must be because Mel and Mir weren't supposed to go this far into the forest and she wants to be a bit dramatic about catching them. Presumably, that's *also* why she's already sent Entile River the coordinates for where they are and left her pocket-com set up so Merlani can call them with one tap without taking their mittens off to say when they're all ready to be picked up and taken back to the lodge where it's warm.

"Well, now!" The human voice chuckles. "That all sounds nice. Do you think this mother of yours would mind if I join you?"

"Sure!" Mel giggles. "Then she and Entile River can help us get you un-lost!"

"And maybe you can help us tell them about the fireflies!" adds Mir.

"*Personally,*" Merlani hears Äiti's voice say in crisply accented Standard as the sounds of her footsteps tell them that she's stepping out of the snow-covered bushes somewhere directly on the other side of the rock, "I'd like to know who you are and why you're out here in the woods alone *before* I go inviting you to tea, yes?"

"Ah, hello, there!" says the human voice. "You must be the mother."

"I am at that, and I'd like my kittens to come here so I can make sure they're not getting frostbitten from leaving their mittens behind as a trail for me to follow." The tone of Äiti's voice is mostly serious now, but wrapped up in cheerful—kind of like when she's occasionally scolded Merlani or one of their littermates for something they shouldn't have done, but more firm.

"Yes, Äiti," chorus Mir and Mel. Merlani hears snow crunching as their littermates get up from somewhere they've been sitting.

The human voice chuckles. "No need to worry, ma'am, I can understand the concern. I'm grateful to your children for showing up when they did. Little Storm here is quite the budding field medic."

"Oh?"

"His leg's *hurt*, Äiti," they hear Mel explain, "but I used our scarves and a nice sturdy stick Sky found to make a splint for him so he can walk back with us!"

"So I can see, Storm." Äiti's voice is approving for a moment, and then goes back to serious-wrapped-in-smiles. "This is the part where you and I exchange names, yes? I'm Ranger Captain Taimri Hämäläinen of the starship *Atascosa*. I can see my kittens have introduced themselves... and you are?"

"Ah, yes, that does explain things." The human doesn't laugh this time so much as he lets out a half of one to accent the sudden awkwardness in his voice. For a moment, Merlani almost wonders if this is because he's afraid of their mother, although they can't imagine why anyone would be. "Thomas E. Milland, graduate student in exoplanetary geology from the Proxima-West Institute for Science and Technology. I'm studying the rock formations in this area for the Interstellar Geological Society as part of my thesis... and had a bit of a mishap a few days ago while I was collecting samples from the top of the ridge back there."

"Which explains the leg?" asks Äiti.

"Which explains the leg. I barely managed to make it back here to my campsite... but my 'com got busted when I fell and I've not managed to repair it to call for assistance."

"And you're out here alone instead of with a team because...?"

"Because I'm a *fool* who likes working in solitude and now deeply regrets not taking anyone up on the offer to come along and distract me." The chuckle comes back into his voice now. "I'd figured if I could hold out a few days someone would notice I hadn't checked in up at the lodge and come looking for me. Never expected to have a miniature Florivan rescue team show up, though."

There's a pause, and then Äiti laughs, the seriousness falling out of her voice altogether. "Okay, Milland, I believe you—and I'd like to hope that these kittens of mine have instincts as good as their entile's as to whether people are trustworthy or not."

"Mister Tom is nice, Äiti!" Mir says.

"Of course he is." She laughs again and calls out a bit louder, "Ocean! You can come join us now! And go ahead and get River on the line for me so I can tell them about this silly geologist your littermates have found."

Merlani does as they're told. When they come around to the other side of the boulder, they see Äiti and their littermates standing in the middle of a bit of a haphazard campsite. Most everything is partially buried in snow, but a small fire is glowing in front of the tent that's set up right against the stone. The unfamiliar voice they've been hearing belongs to a relatively short-looking human man with dark eyes and a deep brown face, all the rest of whom is bundled up in a green and yellow snowsuit. His right leg is splinted and neatly tied up with the pink and purple scarves their littermates had been wearing when they all left the lodge.

Merlani keeps their third eye on him and the campfire, even when they're giving Äiti back her pocket-com so she can talk to their entile.

"Ah!" The new human waves to them cheerfully. "I was wondering where the other sibling these two had mentioned was hiding. Pleased to meet you, Ocean."

Merlani has a bit of an attack of shyness and hugs their Äiti's legs, peering out at the human from behind her. His voice seems nice enough, but they certainly weren't expecting to have to meet new people today.

Äiti pats their head for reassurance, still busy trying to explain the situation to Entile River.

Merlani looks to their two littermates. "We found your mittens," they say softly, still keeping their third eye on the man while they pull the damp bits of pink and purple out of their pockets and hand them to Mir and Mel. "Didn't your hands get cold without them?"

"Oh, kinda!" Mir pulls the bright pink mittens back onto their upper pair of hands. "But then we were holding hands so it wasn't *too* cold, and we still had the liner gloves on. Oh! And we still have the little warmer-pouches in our pockets that Entile River gave us, too."

"But why did you take them *off*?" Merlani shivers a little just thinking about it.

"We were trying to catch one of the fireflies to bring back to you and Äiti!" Mel happily slips the purple mittens back on over their own upper pair of hands.

"Fireflies?" Merlani shivers again.

"Yeah!" Mir giggles. "They're really—"

"Wait, you're *cold* by now, Cinny, aren't you?" Mel interrupts and gives them a hug. "Come sit by the fire with us and Mister Tom and we'll tell you about the fireflies while you warm up."

Merlani nods and lets their littermates lead them over to the warm place in front of the small fire while they all wait for Äiti to finish her conversation with Entile River. By this point, they've decided that if this person is a friend of their littermates, they are also okay with him. Admittedly, they're also desperately curious about why he's here in the mountains alone, almost as much as they are about the "fireflies."

Mel plops down onto the same place on a long supply crate near the campfire where they must have been sitting before and pulls Merlani down to sit beside them. "The fireflies are all gone now," they explain, "but we saw them! They're little snowy floating things that are all green-lit and shiny. They didn't like the mittens, but they'd sit on our hands for a little while after we took them off."

Merlani snuggles up against their littermate as best as they can with their snow clothes in the way. They tilt their head to one side, curious. "I didn't see any of those while we were walking and trying to find you."

"We think they're scared of grown-ups—or maybe humans?" Mir takes the place on Merlani's other side. "They all flew away after they led us to Mister Tom. So they're probably scared of Äiti too."

Merlani considers this for a moment, and then shrugs. They're a bit disappointed to have missed the shiny things, but the explanation makes sense to them. At any rate, they're glad to have located their littermates.

"I've seen the 'fireflies' here and there around my campsite," says Mister Tom, "but to be honest, I thought they might be signs of a concussion or the like until these two showed up and started asking me about them."

"Oh." Merlani nods, still feeling a bit shy and cold.

"He thought *we* were a hallucination at first too," says Mel, proudly, "until I proved I was real by splinting his leg."

"Show them the shiny thing you were looking at when we got here, Mister Tom!" Mir waves excitedly with their re-mittened hands. "Ocean likes stuff like that."

"Is that so?" Mister Tom reaches into a satchel beside him and offers Merlani a bit of stone. "Well, then! Here, Ocean, have a look at this."

As usual, all of Merlani's shyness disappears when presented with interesting minerals. They turn the chunk of rock over in their mitten-covered hands as best as they can, fascinated by the long reddish crystals incorporated into the lightly sparkling white stone.

"It's pretty! You found this here? It looks like the same stone the mountain's made of."

"I did—this is one of the specimens I was collecting when I fell, actually. It's a dolomite marble with a bit of corundum."

"Neat!" Merlani looks more closely at the minerals, now that they know the names of them. "I have a little piece of blue corundum at home that Professor Walton brought back for me the last time they went planetside for a conference! It's not on a matrix like this, though."

"A budding rock hound yourself, then?"

Merlani nods. "Rocks are shiny!"

"So they are." Mister Tom chuckles. "Well, you can keep that one for your collection, then! I have a dozen more from the same place I can use in my research."

"Really?" Merlani turns all three eyes towards him excitedly.

"Of course."

"Thank you very much, Mr. Tom." Merlani makes the most politely thankful bow they can with all of their layers of snow clothes in the way. It *is* a very nice rock, after all. They can't wait to show it to Professor Walton when they get home.

At this point, Äiti comes to join the rest of them by the fire, although she simply stands behind Merlani and their littermates rather than sitting down so they can cuddle with her.

"It's a good thing my kittens found you, Milland," Äiti says, no longer having that serious tone at all in her voice. "My counterpart told me while we were looking for them that we're all to be expecting a bit of a blizzard this evening. You'd have found yourself snowed in for longer than your leg would take to heal, yes?"

"Probably," Mister Tom agrees.

"River also confirmed for me that your lack of checking in with the lodge was noticed, by the way. You're on the list of folks we were asked to pick up before the storm hits."

"Is that so? Well, thank you for coming to get me, then."

"You can thank my counterpart when they get here. In the meantime, I'll help you pack up your campsite. With the snowfall prediction as it is, you won't be able to find this place again until summer."

"I'd appreciate the help, ma'am." Mister Tom slowly gets to his feet, strongly favoring his splinted leg. "It'd take me ages alone just to get the tent down."

"Can we help too?" Mir looks up eagerly at Äiti.

"Hmm... In a few minutes, yes." Äiti reaches down and pats each of their hat-covered heads in turn. "I need the three of you to sit here and keep each other warm for a while first. You've all been out in the snow too long."

"Yes, Äiti," the three of them reply as they scoot closer together.

Merlani, for their part, is perfectly content to sit between their littermates by the fire for a while. Even through their layers, they've started to feel chilled again.

★

MYRVAL IS ALREADY WELL ON THEIR WAY towards their counterpart's coordinates when they pick up her call. They have to hold back a laugh when they hear the explanation of why she's so far away from the lodge.

Leave it to your kittens, Marbree, they think as they fly the rest of the way there. *You're the only other person I know who could find such a perfectly helpful way of avoiding a scolding for getting themself lost.*

Luckily for Myrval, the geologist's camp is in a clearing with plenty of room to set the flitter down. They weren't looking forward to having to trudge through the snow any more than they've already had to today.

"Sorry for the delay," Myrval calls as they step out of the hovering snow-flitter's back door. "The flight path over the ridge is a bit less of a 'shortcut' than the map makes it look."

"Oh, we're in a sheltered enough spot here, yes?" Taimri comes over carrying little Merlani and lifts them up into the flitter. "The kittens have been exchanging stories with their new friend to pass the time."

"Mister Tom knows *lots* of stories about forest-monsters!" Miradyn drags over a rucksack that's almost as big as they are.

"Is that so?" Myrval raises their eyebrows and turns their third eye towards the young geologist their wayward niblings have helped rescue. "I hope the three of you didn't pester him too much."

"We didn't, Entile River," says Miradyn, "promise!"

"Good." Myrval scoops Miradyn up into their arms and sets them into the flitter with little Merlani, then hands the rucksack up to the two kittens. "Now, we've a few other people to pick up, so let's see if we can't get all of Mister Milland's things neat in that front corner so we'll have room."

The two kittens nod enthusiastically and drag the rucksack in.

"Oh, they're better behaved than you give them credit for," says Milland with a grunt as he makes his way over to the flitter. He's limping slowly through the snow. Melbryl is right on his heels helping him carry another bag. "Thank you for the rescue, Ranger. It's much appreciated."

"You *do* know that it's policy most places for field studies to have at *least* three people for safety reasons?" Myrval shakes their head. They pause to help Melbryl up into the snow-flitter with the other kittens. They hand the bags up to the three of them and then look back to the young man. "I'm surprised you were given permission to be out here alone at all."

"Ah, yes, your counterpart reminded me of that too." Milland rubs at the back of his head sheepishly. "And I can see why now. Don't worry, this is my last solo trip for a while I think."

"Good." Myrval gestures at the snow-flitter with both of their left hands. "Now, get on up there. You're *injured*—that makes you part of my cargo now. Tam and I will handle loading the rest of your gear."

"Best not to argue with them," Taimri says before Milland can protest. She carries over a crate and sets it in the flitter for the kitten team to scoot into place. "Storm? You're in charge of keeping an eye on your patient until we get back to the lodge and you can turn him over to their staff nurse."

"Yes, Äiti!" Melbryl beams with excitement and offers Milland their upper pair of hands. "Don't worry, Mister Tom, I'll take good care of you!"

"Well, then, I can't argue with my field medic, now can I?" Milland chuckles and allows the kittens to help him clamber up into the flitter and limp to a seat near the front by his small collection of belongings.

This is yet another of Taimri's excellent skills as both a Ranger and an adoptive parent: being able to convince her charges that staying out of the way and out of trouble is actually *their* idea. Myrval has always appreciated that quality in her.

Kittens and injured geologist sorted, Myrval turns their attention to helping their counterpart load the rest of the young human's gear. Thankfully, there isn't much of it; just another bag holding his tent and climbing equipment and a few boxes of mineral samples.

"So, Jokeni," Taimri asks once the two of them are up in the cockpit of the flitter and taking off from the now-cleared campsite into the lightly snow-filled air above the trees, "how many more lost sheep do we need to bring in before the storm?"

"Two, plus your husband's flock—and lucky for us, no *actual* sheep this time." Myrval passes her the datapad with the names and last reported locations.

"Ah, and here I thought you *liked* the sheep by the end of that mission out at the BC-Tri ag colonies." Taimri gives them a knowing nudge.

"I like sheep just fine, Tam, but *not* when I'm having to ferry them between planets along with a pair of grumpy diplomats." Myrval laughs in spite of themself. That particular mission had ended with the two of them receiving rather nicely-made matching wool sweaters as thanks from the Artisan who had also accompanied the flock of odd fluffy mammals. They may not ever want to play at being a shepherd again, but they do still count it as one of the more memorable adventures they've had since making their compact with a Ranger.

"I do see your point. The sheep were *much* more polite than those two." Taimri laughs with them for a moment and then gestures down the ridge to the south. "Looks like the next campsite on our list is that way."

"All right, *Navigator*," Myrval says, shifting their flight path, "same as always—you handle the maps, I'll handle getting us there."

"I wouldn't have it any other way, Jokeni."

★

"I wouldn't have it any other way, Jokeni."

MERLANI SITS IN THE BACK OF THE FLITTER between their littermates, trying to think warm thoughts. The flitter's inside air is much warmer than outside was, but they still feel cold around their ears and hands.

On one side of Merlani, Mir is carrying on a cheerful conversation about the space station where they all live with the pair of biologists who are perched among the growing collection of camping gear beside Mister Tom. They've taken off their bright pink hat and are adjusting the matching ribbon in their hair that they were wearing underneath it.

On the other side, Mel is making a point of watching their patient closely, as if concerned that he'll get hurt again if they turn their eyes away. They too have set their hat aside, neatly laying all four of their mittens on top of it for safekeeping. Mister Tom seems to find Mel's junior medic fussiness endearing.

Merlani has the little bit of stone the nice geologist gave them nestled in between their lower pair of hands. They slowly turn it over and over, hindered somewhat by the thickness of the mittens they're still wearing. Their littermates might think the liner gloves are sufficient now that they're out of the snow, but Merlani doesn't. They've just barely started to thaw out the bits of them that were getting chilled; removing any of their layers at all is unappealing. Their cozy hat is also still on. It might muffle their ears a bit, but it does keep the warmth in.

Marble, Merlani thinks, focusing their warm thoughts towards the things they've learned from helping the Geology professors back home, *that's metamorphic... so heat and pressure. You were deep inside the mountains once before they were ever mountains, and you got all squished.* Merlani is somewhat familiar with the feeling of being squished. At the moment, Mer and Mel are close enough to them to be almost a squishing force. They don't really mind it, most of the time. Right now, it's quite nice. Being squished in the middle of their littermates means being *warm*, and that's been a constant for as long as they can remember.

And dolomite is... limestone's cousin? That's right, isn't it? Merlani is just cold enough still that they can't quite remember.

Merlani's about to speak up and ask their littermates' new friend about how he thinks the rock in their hands was made, but their mother's cheerful voice from the flitter's cockpit interrupts them.

"Stand by for a landing back there," she calls, "and get ready to make some room for our last batch of passengers."

Merlani slips their rock back into one of their puffy snow jacket's pockets. It takes a bit of doing, since they're still wearing the jacket and it makes their arms a bit hard to move. One of Dad's most important rules about landings is that anything that could hurt if it hit someone has to be secured well before turbulence or gravity gets a chance to throw it.

Even though the flitter sets down gently into the snow, Mir still makes a point of wrapping their nearest upper arm around Merlani's shoulders while they're landing to hold them secure. Mir's always been the sort to worry about things like them somehow getting bumped out of their seat. Merlani doesn't mind. They don't like the idea of being a potential projectile any more than they'd assume the rock in their pocket would.

As soon as the flitter lands, Äiti appears to open the big back door. "Sky, Storm? Help our new friends make room for everyone. It's about to be a bit snug in here, yes?"

"Yes, Äiti!" the two of them chorus, hopping up from their seats. Merlani does their best to scoot over as far as they can towards the front of the flitter so more people can fit in too.

As the big back door of the flitter's combined cargo and passenger area slides open, it reveals a group of snow-dusted people in mostly matching grey outfits. Right in the front of the group is a man with a rather bushy beard that's also dusted with snowflakes. He's a welcome sight if ever there was one.

"Dad!" Mir excitedly forgets about the box they were helping Mel scoot towards the front of the flitter and bounces out into the snow to hug him. "We missed you!"

For his part, Dad laughs and spins the hug around in a circle before depositing Mir back into the flitter. "Great Scott, but I missed you too, Sky!" He hops up after them and leans in to give Äiti a brief whiskery kiss on the cheek. "All of you! Thanks for coming to pick us up, love. The snow doesn't seem all that hospitable this afternoon."

"Lucky for you, I know a place with a nice fireplace." Äiti makes a little shooing motion towards the front of the flitter. "Now get out of the way so we can load up your poor cadets and go back there, yes?"

"Yes, Ms. Ranger," says Dad playfully, "whatever you say."

Mir pulls on Dad's hand and leads him up to where Merlani is sitting. "Here, Dad," they say, "You can sit with Cinny—that way everyone will fit, and they can help you thaw out."

"I could do with some thawing. Let's see..." Dad slides into the seat and helps Merlani scoot into his lap. "Probably need two more kittens sitting with me to thaw properly."

Mir and Mel happily take their spots on either side of him while the cadets all file in. Soon, the back of the flitter is filled with people and backpacks, only leaving a very narrow path down the middle.

The pair of cadets entering last exchange a glance and then look up to Äiti. "Ma'am," says the one Merlani recognizes now as the nice Miss Ionescu who always has lemon sweets in her pocket to share. She's pitching her voice into a stage whisper. "The whole survival training exercise is over now, isn't it?"

"I'd say so," Äiti replies.

"Good. That means we don't have to be subjected to the 'Ambassador' anymore. We were all starting to get a bit sick of him."

"Oh?" Äiti shakes her head mirthfully as she closes and secures the flitter's back door. "Was George an ambassador this time, then? I thought he was going to be an overeager scientist."

"Ambassador, ma'am... and he's *your* problem now."

"That he is." Äiti laughs and gives Miss Ionescu a pat on the shoulder. "And I will be keeping him. Even if he is a bit of a ham sometimes, yes?"

"Oh, now, Tam, don't let them go telling stories. I do a *good* ambassador impression!" Dad grins up at her as she walks by.

"He talked Ionescu and Noble into *carrying* him the last three kilometers today, Ma'am," says Cadet Gravener, who's now sitting on the other side of Mir. "And he got that song about the fish stuck in all of our heads, too."

Äiti turns before she climbs the three steps up to the cockpit door. "Did you really, George?" She raises an eyebrow at him.

"Well... windy weather and all, you know how it is." Dad chuckles softly. Merlani can feel the familiar rumble of it through all of their layers as he hugs them a little closer. "They did ask me to stop remembering all of my songs about ice and snow, after all."

"I can't imagine why." Äiti looks back to Miss Ionescu and Mr. Noble. "I'd say I owe you both a big cup of coffee for humoring my husband… and for keeping him out of trouble. You'll remind me when we get back to the lodge, yes?"

"Yes, Ma'am," says Mr. Noble, saluting primly.

"Taimri," calls Entile River, continuing in Äiti's native language, "do you have our cargo settled down yet? The wind's picking up and I don't want to let this storm get any closer with us out in it."

"All ready to go!" Äiti hops up the steps and disappears into the flitter's cockpit.

Merlani looks up at their father and snuggles back against him. "You're all fuzzy, Dad."

Dad rubs a hand over his beard thoughtfully. "It does seem that way. You warm enough, Cinna-bun?"

Merlani nods. Now that the door's closed again, the chilly snow-laden breeze that came in with everyone is gone. Not to mention that they're sitting on their father's lap, and he's warm even through his snowsuit.

After a moment, Entile River leans out of the cockpit door and beckons towards them with one hand. "And just what do you think you're doing, George?"

"Catching up on my kitten snuggle quota?"

Entile River rolls all three eyes. "There's a *blizzard* setting in."

"Great Scott, is there? I *never* would have guessed." Dad drawls the words out in that particular dry teasing tone he saves specifically for Entile River.

"Just get up here and fly us out of it, will you?"

Dad stands, picking Merlani up as he does and turning to set them back into the seat. "Fine, fine, half a moment."

"Can I stay with you?" Merlani looks up at him with pleading eyes. "You're *warm*."

Dad nods, scooting out of the way so their mother can slip back down the steps and into the seat between Mir and Mel. Normally, Merlani would prefer sitting with her, since she's gone so often, but they haven't seen their father in what feels like a long time and they were just getting comfortable. He carries them up into the cockpit.

"You don't like the look of the wind, then?" he asks Entile River quietly once the partition door between the cockpit and the rear portion of the flitter has slid shut behind him.

"I don't. It's been rough since we picked up the biologists, and it's getting worse." Entile River plops themself into the copilot's seat and gestures to the controls. "I'd rather have the expert get us through it."

"Right." Dad nods and settles down into the pilot's chair, adjusting it to account for his height and then arranging Merlani in his lap so he can hold them without them being in the way. He unzips the front of his jacket and tucks the flaps of it around Merlani before zipping just the bottom bit of it back up to keep it in place. "Hang on, then, I'll have us back in front of that fire you kept sending me pictures of in no time."

"You're sure don't want to sit with your mother?" Entile River tilts their head to Merlani curiously while the flitter's rising up out of the snow.

"Dad's *warm*." Merlani answers, simply. They'd missed his warmth a lot more than they'd realized.

"Point taken."

"All right, we're above the trees... what heading for the lodge, River?"

Entile River pulls up the map on their copilot's display. "North by northwest—right on the other side of that ridge there." They gesture in the appropriate direction.

"Got it."

Merlani makes themself comfortable and watches the sky and the drifting snow and the mountains go by. They're not worried, even when the wind shakes the flitter a bit. They've spent their whole life flying with their father. They have no doubt at all that they're safe.

★

An hour or so later, Merlani and their siblings sit cuddled together under a blanket on one of the couches in front of the lodge's big windows, watching the heavy flakes of snow falling outside. Ever since they got back with all of the people Äiti and Entile River had needed to find, the snow has been getting heavier and the wind stronger.

It's nice to watch, but Merlani is *very* glad not to be out in the cold anymore. Their ears and hands have finally started to feel properly thawed out now.

"We never did get to finish our snow-person." Mir shakes their head in a way that makes the bow they wear behind their ears wiggle.

"No," Mel agrees, "but the fireflies were neat!"

"I still didn't get to see any of them," Merlani says softly, fighting off sleepiness that's growing between all of the excitement of the day being over and the feelings of warmth and safety that being snuggled in between their littermates like this sparks.

Mir brightens. "Maybe once the storm is over we can all go look for them again! Entile River did say we'd be here an extra few days because of it..."

Merlani smiles, looking out into the windblown snow that's currently being lit up outside the window by the lodge's porch lights. "That would be fun."

"Room for one more in that blanket, kittens?" Dad appears behind the couch with a tray of steaming mugs. His ruddy-pale face is framed by dark-with-grey-flecks hair and a beard that's *much* more fluffy than it was when he left with his students for the big hike a week ago. Merlani is particularly glad to have him back, considering how cold it is outside and how much warmer the family nest is when their whole family is in it.

"Make that two!" Äiti appears right behind him with a basket of the lodge's famous ginger-spice cookies.

The kittens happily scoot together into the middle of the couch to make room for their parents, then each accept a mug of honey-sweetened tea and a cookie. Dad takes another of the soft striped blankets from the basket beside the couch before he sits down beside Mir. He passes one end of it to Äiti once she's taken her place next to Mel so the two of them can spread it over everyone's legs.

"See any more of your fireflies out there, kittens?" Äiti takes a sip from her coffee and nods her head in the direction of the window.

"No, but I *know* they're out there." Mir pauses to readjust the bow in their hair. "Maybe they don't like being out in blizzards either?"

"Maybe," says Dad, reaching over to ruffle Mir's ears. He reaches over and does the same to Mel and Merlani as well, just for good measure. "A couple of my students told me they thought they saw something similar hanging around, but there's nothing on the books *officially* about a native life form like your fireflies that I've been able to find. Considering that they led you to someone who was hurt and needed help, though? I'd like to think that they're friendly little snow-bugs, whatever they are."

A few minutes later, Entile River reappears too and takes their usual spot on the middle part of the couch with Merlani rearranged to be sitting in their lap. That's the one good thing about being the smallest, as far as Merlani cares: they always get to be the one who's right in the middle when everyone's together like this. The middle is the best spot for soaking up family warmth.

"Well," says Entile River, pausing to take a long sip from their own steaming cup of minty water. "I will admit, this is nice—although next time the two of you decide to arrange a 'family vacation,' can we try for somewhere *warm*?"

"What, River," quips Dad, "you don't want to play snowbirds anymore?"

"I don't like being cold on the *ground* anymore than I like being cold up in space. You know that." Entile River chuckles. Merlani can feel the laughter vibrating into their back. "Even so, there's going to be a snowball with your name on it once this storm clears, George Barker, just when you least expect it."

"Oh, now, it's been *ages* since I've been part of a proper snowball fight!" Dad grins through the fluff of his beard. "I'll take you up on that offer."

"All right, then. You can have Sky and Storm on your team... *I* get Taimri."

"Sounds fair enough. Tam's practically a team on her own, of course, but I'd say the kittens are a good match for *you*." Dad's still using his good-natured teasing voice. He and Entile River are always teasing each other like this.

Entile River matches his tone. "And of course, I'll have to invite those poor cadets of yours to join my team too... I'm sure they'd be up for tossing the odd snowball your way."

"What about me?" Merlani asks, pausing in the middle of nibbling on their cookie to look up between their father and entile. They don't know how to feel about their name being left out of the team-choosing for this 'snow fight' game.

"*You*, little Ocean, get to keep score and make sure your father doesn't get too competitive and do silly things like tossing people into snow drifts like he did the last time I let him and your mother involve me in a snowball fight. It's a very important job." Entile River sets their lower pair of arms around Merlani and gives them a reassuring hug. "I'll see about finding you a score-keeper whistle and everything."

Merlani considers it for a moment, then nods their acceptance. They still don't know what the game *is*, but if potentially getting eaten by a snow drift again is part of it, they like the idea of being the one with the whistle instead.

Dad laughs and gives Entile River's shoulder an affectionate nudge. "Now, River, really, *you're* the one who shook all the snow off of a tree on top of me first..."

"That wasn't entirely me," Entile River protests, obviously holding back a laugh. "I just climbed up the thing and helped shake it. Dropping snow on you was *Ocean's* idea."

"Now *that*, I believe." Dad shakes his head. "Breezy was the one who started that whole snowball fight in the first place, now that I think about it."

"To be fair," Äiti says, giggling, "I *may* have shown them how to make snowballs just to see if they'd throw one at you."

"Of course you did." Dad's voice takes on a familiar sort of nostalgic sadness, after a moment. "They'd have liked this place."

"They would," Entile River agrees, matching his tone perfectly. "Ocean always did have the oddest taste in places to visit."

"And in people?" asks Dad, still with that same tone but with a touch of his usual sense of humor shining through.

"*Especially* in people." Entile River flicks their ears pointedly, then softens their tone. "Don't worry, though, George, I *have* come to the conclusion that they were right about you, you know."

"I know."

The adults grow quiet, sipping from their drinks and watching the snow.

Merlani and their littermates share a look. Dad doesn't talk about their Nida as much during the long times Äiti and Entile River are off away from home doing Ranger things. None of them had ever heard about family snowball fights before this. He's told the three of them more as they've gotten older, of course, and they all know that Merlani's own public name was given to them because they look so much like a miniature version of their parent.

Still, there's a lot more that they don't know—especially from when their parent first made the Navigator's compact with him.

Dad and Entile River both tend to get quiet like this whenever a conversation turns that direction. When Merlani and their littermates have asked Äiti why this is, since *she* doesn't mind talking about things at all, she's always answered that there are a lot of things that both of them have been through that make remembering hurt, even if the memories are of good things. None of the kittens quite understand this, but they all believe her that eventually they'll be old enough to be told all the stories that are waiting for them.

Normally, by now, Mir or Mel would have asked some question about the confusing conversation the adults are having in order to hopefully get more of the story out of them. Curiosity, though, is no match for the power of a long and eventful day to induce sleepy contentment.

By the time the three adults have started talking to each other again, Merlani and their littermates are all well asleep and purring happily, cuddled up in the center of their family. They don't even wake when they're carried up to their family's guest room and tucked in together into a proper nest for the night.

Outside, the snow falls and billows on the wind, refreshing the thick blanket of white over the mountains. The half-finished form of a certain snow-person is buried before long in a soft drift all its own to await its makers return. Scattered remains of campsites, too, are neatly swept clean by the wind and dusted with a fresh layer of snow. No one but perhaps the trees themselves could say for sure where any tracks from the people who passed by the day before might be. The trees would hardly care to say, though, and nor would the creatures of the mountains who slumber in the burrows amidst their roots.

If a few small green-glittering sparks of light happen to peer in through the windows of the lodge in the night to make sure that all of the odd guests to their forest are safely within its walls, no one notices. Here, in this one small oasis of warmth, all is well and calm in the midst of the blizzard.

★ THE END ★

APPENDIX

Timeline of *Strange Space™ Adventures*

The following timeline lists all of the published *Strange Space™ Adventures* and Short Stories in roughly chronological order. Where stories feature major time skips, they have been placed based on the earliest events of that story.

Short Stories marked with *[1] can be found in *Tales of the Navigators: Volume 1.*

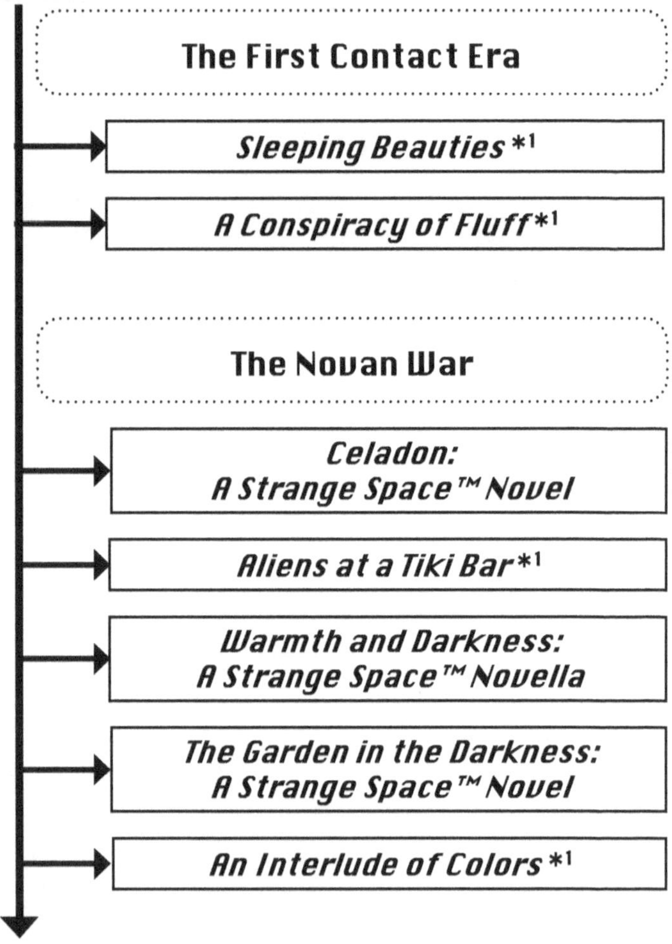

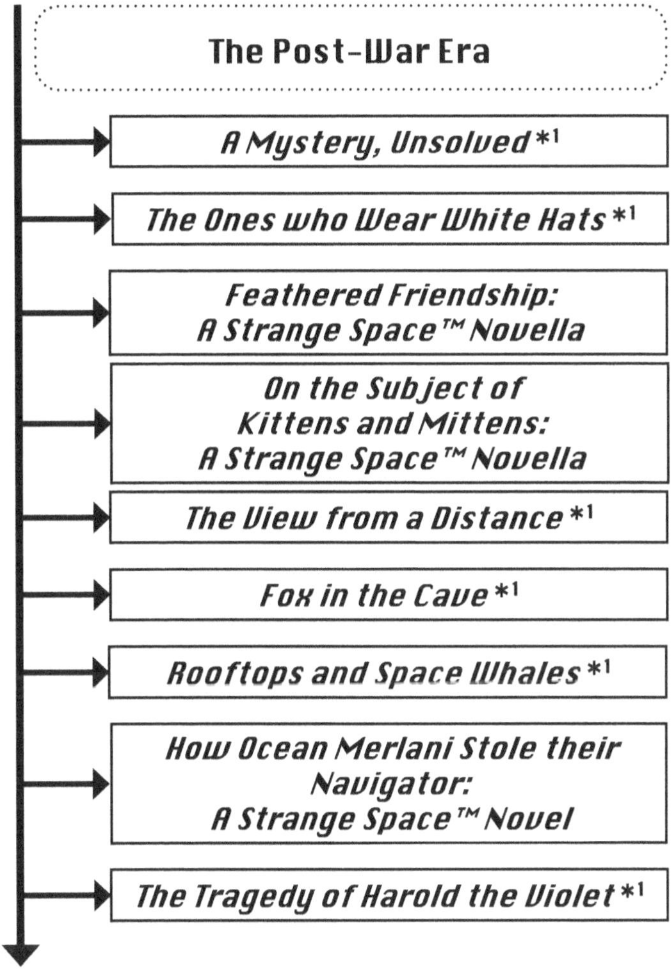

The Post-War Era

A Mystery, Unsolved [1]

The Ones who Wear White Hats [1]

*Feathered Friendship:
A Strange Space™ Novella*

*On the Subject of
Kittens and Mittens:
A Strange Space™ Novella*

The View from a Distance [1]

Fox in the Cave [1]

Rooftops and Space Whales [1]

*How Ocean Merlani Stole their
Navigator:
A Strange Space™ Novel*

The Tragedy of Harold the Violet [1]

On Character Identities and Pronouns

On the Subject of Kittens and Mittens takes place in a far future setting in which human society has long since reached the stage of accepting and celebrating all varieties of diversity. This is a sort of world that I, personally, would like to live in. I don't claim it to be a *perfect* setting, but I do take an optimistic view of our potential as a species.

Several of the human characters presented in this story would, in today's terms, likely identify with one or more communities under the LGBTQIA+ umbrella. While the narrative of this story did not call for these characters to specifically state which labels they would use, and I like to imagine that a lot of who they are can be inferred through their interactions, as a member of the LGBTQIA+ community *myself*, I'm aware of the importance of clear representation. Seeing characters like ourselves in stories where they are valued for who they are and able to live without being marginalized for their nature is, in my opinion, *powerful*, and a big part of my philosophy as a writer.

Please note that at the same time, it is impossible to represent an entire community in the form of one character. My characters are simply themselves, and while they draw on my own experiences and those of people I know, they are not meant to be "perfect" renditions of one thing or another. Just like every human, their various identities are *aspects* of them, rather than the entirety of their personality.

That all being said, the following characters central to this story would like to "come out" to you and share this aspect of their lives:

Thomas E. Milland would describe himself as aromantic, but generally attracted to women.

Raven Kirsch would describe themself as agender.

On behalf of all of my characters, I'd like to thank you, dear reader, for being accepting of them and respecting their preferred sets of pronouns.

I hope that we all will one day live in a world like the one these characters inhabit, in which a person can openly be themself without fear. I do believe it's possible for us to get there, too; every small step we make in the right direction matters.

—*Katie Silverwings*

On Academy Survival Training Excursions

As part of their standard cirriculum, the various space service academies of the Sol Coalition include practical education in wilderness and extreme condition survival. While this is optional for many courses of study, it is a required element of all Command, Flight, and Astral Navigation/Quantum Space Drive Engineering programs. In theory, students in these areas would, in the course of their space service careers, be the ones most likely to be in charge of leading any group of survivors of an emergency situation. Tactical pilots, in particular, are considered highly likely to find themselves in need of survival skills in the event they survive an unexpected landing far from civilization.

In addition to the academic aspects of the survival training curriculum, students are requried to attend a minimum of one survival training excursion per year of their course of study. Typically, students of all levels from one department attend the same excursion, which is led by their course's head instructors. Students opting in to survival training are placed with these course-specific groups as needed, or formed into a mixed group depending on how many of them are participating in a given year. Students who are dual- or multi-specialist may be requried to attend multiple survival training excursions, depending on which departments they belong to.

Students training for advanced certification in Field Medicine are a unique case, as they do not attend a department-specific survival training excursion. Instead, in their first year they are divided between the academy's other excursion groups. After that, they are expected to join a minimum of two excursion groups each year until they graduate. This both allows these students to gain experience working with their peers from different departments and ensures that there are trained medics included in each group.

Lasting between one and two weeks each, the survival training excursions take place in a wide variety of uninhabited regions of whatever planets or life-supporting moons are local to the academy in question. Usually, the location is rotated from year to year so that students are exposed to a wide variety of conditions and scenarios. In many cases, one of the instructors will act the part of an injured or uncooperative person whom the group will have to care for during their journey.

An additional mixed-department excursion is held each academic year for all of the graduating senior students, which is run as an active simulation. During this "final exam", the students are dropped off at their starting point as if they have just survived a crash landing and are expected to find their way to a specified pick-up point. They are remotely monitored by their instructors during the excersise, and graded based on their performance both individually and as a group.

These survival training excursions are seen as both a means of preparing students for potential emergency situations and as a crucial bonding excersise for the members of a particular department. In some programs, the annual survival training hike is seen as a right of passage as much as an educational experience.

On Florivan Names

Florivan names consist of two parts: the 'public' name and the 'personal' name. The 'personal' or 'kitten-name' is given to a Florivan when they first open their eyes, while the 'public' name is chosen for them when they are old enough to be presented to the Council of Elders. Some kittens receive one or the other half of their name in honor of one of their ancestors or entiles, which has become more common since the end of the Novan War. Storm Melbryl, Sky Miradyn, and Ocean Merlani, for example, were given their public names in honor of their grandparent, entile, and parent, respectively.

Personal names come from the ancestral Florivan language, and are largely untranslatable. All of the kittens in a litter will usually be given names with the same or similar initial sounds.

Public names are always words from human languages which connect somehow to the individual's coloring. Kittens, therefore, receive their public names once they have shed enough of their fur to show a large patch of a recognizable color. Elders will often carry a theme through the public names of their kittens such as different stones, plants, or a specific language of origin.

Florivans are most often addressed by their public names. Only Elders, family members, or the closest of friends will address or talk about a Florivan by their personal name, and then only in private. (Private, in this case, also extends to situations where only other Florivans or close friends of the family are present.)

Florivans also commonly take on nicknames which are used by their families, friends, and colleagues. Who can use a certain nickname for them depends on the situation and origin of the nickname. River Myrval, for example, is called "Jokeni" only by their counterpart, while their sibling Ocean Marbree was called "Breezy" by both their Navigator and most of the people they worked with.

Florivan Elders are addressed formally with their title, although most of them will grant close friends and colleagues permission to address them by their public name alone outside of formal situations. Younger members of an Elder's line will call them 'Nida' ('Parent') or 'Ai-Nida' ('Grandparent') as appropriate in most situations. Apprentices to an Elder typically use their title as a sign of respect regardless of whose line they belong to, although the Elder may ask them to do otherwise in private.

Katie Silverwings is an award-winning author, glassblower, and artisan originally from Texas and now a nomadic creative spirit. She holds a BA in English and History from McMurry University in Abilene, Texas, with minors in Art, Arts Administration, and Biblical Greek Translation, as well as a BA (Hons.) in Glass from the University for the Creative Arts in the UK. Silverwings identifies as aromantic, asexual, and genderfae; "she/her", "they/them", and "fae/faer" pronouns are all welcome.

Long fascinated by nature and space, Silverwings' speculative fiction work centers around notions of optimistic futurism, friendship, found family, and adventurous journeys into the known and unknown. Her characters do most of the driving, and she does her best to keep up and negotiate pleasing stories with them.

Silverwings' two cats are commonly found staring over her shoulder while she's writing. The small cloud of dark matter with eyes likes to sit in her lap and interfere with typing, while the calico makes operatic editorial comments from across the room.

www.KatieSilverwings.com
@KatieSilverwings

MORE BOOKS
BY KATIE SILVERWINGS

Celadon

✦ A Strange Space™ Novel ✦

The Novan War has just begun. All that stands between Humanity and utter destruction are the ships of the Sol Coalition Defense Fleet.

The only problem? None of those ships are equipped with the all-important Quantum Space Drive which allows humanity to travel between planets and stars at a reasonable scale of time. The Drive needs Florivan QSD Engineers to run it, and Florivans are pacifists. Their Council of Elders has never allowed service on military vessels.

The Fleet can do little more than sit at the edges of the Coalition's seven member systems and *wait* for the Novans to attack.

Celadon Toreval is the Youngest of the Florivan Council of Elders. If anyone can come to Fleet Admiral Marvin's aid and help her save her people—and theirs—it's them.

Celadon, though, has their own reasons to get involved...

Available now from Amazon and Barnes & Noble and at
www.KatieSilverwings.com

Warmth and Darkness

The Garden in the Darkness

How Ocean Merlani Stole their Navigator

Tales of the Navigators (Volume 1)

Feathered Friendship

✶ A Strange Space™ Novella ✶

Dr. Ariadne Salzar-Newman is *not* a mad scientist.

She *is* a scientist—a brilliant one at that—but she's hardly *mad*. If one asks MSS *Venture's* staff psychologist and QSD Engineer, the Florivan Elder Navy Irleeim, she's only "amusingly eccentric, with a bit more of a fascination with the Strange than is healthy for a human."

That fascination has her once again working with the dangerous miasmas of Quantum Space, in hopes of making travel through that veiled dimension safer for human starships. It's not particularly safe for a scientist, for sure. Still, having taken Navy's apprentice under her wing as a part-time assistant, she's safer than usual. Working with her is good for Cobalt Mereday, too, if only because her unique brand of oddity seems to be the only thing capable of helping them.

Even Dr. Salzar-Newman has no reason to suspect just how much of an effect this particular project will have on her family and her protégé, nor how far-reaching the consequences will be.

Little Bernadette is *not* an ordinary budgerigar...

9 781959 922308